YESTERDAY'S RAIN

YESTERDAY'S RAIN

KIM SIGAFUS

7th GENERATION
Summertown, Tennessee

Library of Congress Cataloging-in-Publication Data available upon request.

© 2022 by Kim Sigafus

Cover and interior design: John Wincek

7th Generation
Book Publishing Company
PO Box 99, Summertown, TN 38483
888-260-8458
bookpubco.com
nativevoicesbooks.com

ISBN: 978-1-939053-42-8

27 26 25 24 23 22   1 2 3 4 5 6 7 8 9

*C*hildren aren't born bullies. Their world teaches them how to behave. Bullying is the result of deeply buried anger and frustration, combined with lost hope. This book is dedicated to all who are unable to express themselves. May we learn how to hear and listen what is said and what is unsaid. When we listen, we learn. When we learn, we become better people.

CONTENTS

Unexpected Visit

S ydney sat in her bedroom on the bed with her pillow in her lap. Her father was in the living room talking with her mother, and Sydney wanted no part of the conversation.

It had been six months since the judge ruled in her mother's favor and her father was made to adhere to the supervised visitation decree. He was angry for a long time, and after the first several visits with the court liaison, he almost lost his right to see her at all. He finally and reluctantly agreed to anger management counseling and had been going for several months before he called her mother and asked for this visit. He didn't want to see Sydney, he said; he wanted to clear the air with her mother.

Sydney sighed as curiosity got the better of her. She leaned forward, trying to hear some of the conversation now, but the voices were low. There was no yelling or rude comments, and Sydney frowned, wondering what her father might be muttering under his breath for her mother to hear.

After a moment she sat back, settling herself against the headboard of her bed. A moment later, there was a knock on the door.

"Yes?"

"Can I come in, please?"

It was her father. Automatic defense mechanisms kicked in, and Sydney tensed up, grabbing the pillow and hugging it to her chest. When she didn't respond, she heard her father sigh.

"I just want to apologize," he said, and Sydney considered that for a moment before deciding to get up and answer the door.

Her father stood in the doorway, his head down and his hands in his pockets. He had cut his hair, and it was now neatly combed around his face. He had dark brown eyes, which regarded her thoughtfully as he raised his head to look at her.

"Is it all right if I come in?" he asked, searching her eyes.

"I thought you weren't here to see me."

He nodded. "It was your mother's idea."

"You aren't supposed to see me unless you go through the court liaison."

"I know. Your mother thought a few minutes would be okay." He looked down at the floor again. "Is it all right?"

Sydney backed up and allowed him into her bedroom. He entered, glancing around with a smile. "You always were the neatest teenager I ever knew," he said. "You always kept your room so clean and tidy."

Sydney frowned. She had never heard him pay her a compliment before. Not trusting it, she brushed it aside and sat back down on the bed and waited.

He stood in the middle of the room until she gestured to a chair by her little desk. He sat down and then turned to look at her.

"I couldn't believe what you said to me at court that day," he began, and she tensed up again. "You should never talk to your parents that way. We deserve your respect."

Sydney opened her mouth to respond but stopped when he held up a hand.

"But I want to thank you for that conversation."

Sydney closed her mouth and frowned. "What? I don't understand." She crossed her legs and pulled her pillow even tighter to her chest. "You're not mad about that?"

"Oh, I was plenty mad at the time. It took me a long time to calm down about it. But after three or four visits with you that didn't go so well, the liaison took me aside and gave me an ultimatum. Either I did something about my anger issues, or she was going to tell the judge I was a threat to your mental health."

Her father sat back in the chair and sighed. "She said to not make another appointment to see you until I decided what I was going to do." Sydney watched him look back down at the floor. "I have to admit, someone telling me what to do is not my favorite thing, even if I know deep down they are right."

Sydney remained silent, and her father glanced up at her. "Don't you have anything to say about all this?" he asked.

She shrugged. "I'm waiting for the apology."

He stared at her for a moment and then reluctantly smiled. "You don't mince words," he said. "Just like Nokomis."

"I miss her."

"Have you talked to her since you moved?" He grimaced. "My mother would smack me upside the head for my behavior toward you and Dakotah."

"Yup."

He laughed now, and Sydney was struck by how handsome he really was. She had never gotten past the scowl on his face to figure out why her mother had chosen to marry him.

As the pain of past taunts and jabs flitted through her memory, she sat back and looked away. She didn't trust this man in front of her who seemed to have seen the light of day in regard to his behavior. He had hurt her over and over again with his words, making sure she could never accept that she was fine the way she was. She had to be better, faster, smarter . . .

"Sydney?"

She glanced over at him but didn't speak, choosing instead to wait and hear him out.

"I'm so sorry for the way I have treated you," he said. "Your mother says I made you feel like you were never enough, and that wasn't the case." He ran a hand through his hair and sighed. "I guess I don't give out a lot of compliments. All you ever heard were harsh words."

Sydney remained quiet, and he went on.

"I am trying to change. I have been this way a long time, and I suspect it will take a long time to change the bad habits and adopt a different way of thinking about things." He caught her gaze and gave her an earnest smile.

"But I want to change. I want to be a good father to you." He looked away then. "I've already lost the only woman I have ever loved. I can't lose you too."

He leaned forward in his chair and reached out for her hand, which she did not give him.

"Please say you'll give me a chance to prove myself," he said. "I know you will need time to process everything, and I won't push you. I will keep to the visitation schedule until the next court date, and then you can make the decision whether or not I need to see you with the liaison present, okay?"

Sydney caught his gaze and held it until he became uncomfortable. Then she nodded.

Relieved, he nodded back and then got up and headed for the door. "I will see you soon, all right?"

Sydney nodded, and he opened the door and left, closing it softly behind him.

He found his ex-wife in the kitchen, washing dishes. She turned when she heard him enter the room.

"How did it go?" she asked, wiping her hands on a towel.

"It was tough," he said. "She's a hard one."

Dakotah nodded. "You've hurt her."

"Yes."

"She doesn't trust you. You will have to prove yourself."

"To you as well?"

Dakotah shook her head. "It's too late for that."

"I love you . . ."

"And I you. But sometimes that's not enough. Some people aren't meant to be together."

He was silent for a moment as his eyes took in her long black hair, neatly tied up and secured with a beaded turtle barrette. She was so brave and caring, which had captivated him from the start. It had taken him a while to fall in love with her, but she had snuck into his heart and now held it in her hand.

"Roger?" asked Dakotah, uncomfortable with the way he was looking at her now.

He turned to go. "Thanks for letting me say my piece," he said, "and for letting me see Sydney."

"I hope it helped you guys," she replied, and he nodded.

"Me too."

He left quietly, pulling the door closed behind him. Sydney came out of her room, still tightly hugging her pillow to her chest, and entered the kitchen.

"So?" she asked.

"So?"

Sydney shrugged. "We'll see."

"I guess so. By the way, Finn called. You left your phone out here. I didn't answer it, but I thought he left a message."

"Okay, thanks." Sydney grabbed her phone and went back to her room, shutting the door.

Dakotah glanced at Sydney's door and then the front door her ex-husband had exited out of. Then she turned back to her dishes.

She sure hoped they could work it out. While she didn't have it in her at the moment to forgive him, she thought maybe Sydney did.

Old Habits
Die Hard

Finn sat across from Sydney in the school cafeteria, grinning. He had just stuck his finger in the pudding on his tray.

"I finally found something good to eat," he declared, then glanced over at her pudding. "Ah . . . are you gonna eat that?"

"What's wrong with your beef stew?" asked Sydney, shoving a spoonful of her own stew into her mouth. "I like it."

"I don't, and I'm hungry." Finn sat forward. "I'll trade you."

"Are you going to eat my pudding with your fingers?"

"Nope."

"Then why didn't you use a spoon with your pudding?"

"What if I didn't like it?" Finn shook his head. "Then there would have been icky pudding all over my spoon."

"What does that matter if you're not going to use it to eat anything else?"

"Look, are you going to trade me pudding for beef stew or not?" Finn placed his hand over his heart. "I'm wasting away over here."

Sydney rolled her eyes and pushed her tray over to him. He made a point of picking up his spoon and then ate the pudding right off of the tray.

"I love me some butterscotch pudding," he said, licking his spoon clean. When Sydney smiled, he pushed his tray toward her.

"Here you go," he said.

She leaned over, scooped the stew from his tray to hers, and then pushed his tray back.

He shook his head. "You sure are a dainty one," he remarked.

Sydney laughed. "That's a word no one has ever used to describe me."

"You could have eaten it right off my tray."

"Eww . . ."

"Like I said . . . dainty."

Sydney rolled her eyes again and shook her head. She finished the stew and then glanced over at him.

"Are you done?" she asked.

"I was pretty much done before I started eating," he replied, getting up.

"Well then, let's go."

Sydney picked up her tray, and Finn followed her to the tray disposal. As Sydney turned the corner to put the tray away, she bumped into Amelia and Maci. Amelia's milk spilled all over the pair and started dripping off them and onto the floor.

"What the . . . oh, it's you," said Amelia as she bent over to pick up the empty milk carton. She was dripping wet with milk. "Figures."

Silently, Finn handed Maci his napkins, and she took them without saying a word. She tried in vain to wipe herself down.

Amelia dumped the scraps on her and Maci's trays in the garbage before setting the trays on the conveyor belt to the kitchen. Then she turned around and pulled her purple designer shirt out to look at it.

"Of course, it is ruined now," she said to no one in particular, and Sydney frowned.

"It's just wet," she replied. "If you tried to wipe it down . . ."

"And make it worse?" Amelia laughed. "No, I don't think so. This is silk."

"I'm sorry . . . ," Sydney started, but Amelia put up a hand to stop her.

"I hope your mother has a job, rez girl," she said, "because she's going to have to pay for this shirt."

"It can probably be dry-cleaned," said Finn, dumping his tray and then reaching for Sydney's.

Amelia gave him a cold stare. "Well, either way, I'm not going to pay for it."

"It's not that big of a deal," said Sydney. "Just get it cleaned."

"Considering the secondhand clothes you wear, you obviously don't have a clue how to clean expensive clothes," said Maci, handing back the wadded-up wet napkins to Finn. He grimaced and then took them, tossing them into the garbage.

Finn glanced over at Sydney and saw her clench her jaw.

"Come on, Sydney," he said quickly. "Let's go."

Sydney ignored him. "Shut up, Maci," she said. "Your ignorance is astounding. You wouldn't know fashion or style if it hit you on the head. If Amelia didn't tell you what to wear, you'd come to school looking like a stew bum."

She and Finn turned to go, but Amelia reached out and grabbed her shirt.

"You're responsible for my ruined shirt," said Amelia, raising her voice now. "And you're going to pay for it."

Sydney turned and started to walk away. Amelia's eyes narrowed, and she went after Sydney, grabbing her arm and whipping her around.

That was it. Finn saw the look on Sydney's face, but it was too late to do anything. He watched her step forward and go toe-to-toe with Amelia.

Sydney snickered. "If you think I'm going to pay for that dollar-store piece of cloth you call a shirt, you can think again," she spat out, taking another step toward Amelia. "You better leave me alone if you know what's good for you. I've had enough of your crap."

Amelia laughed, glancing around nervously. "You obviously have no idea who you're dealing with," she said, and Sydney gave her a threatening smile.

"You have no idea who *you're* dealing with. Come near me again and I'll make sure you regret it."

"You don't scare me."

"Then you're stupid, and I have no time for stupid people."

Sydney turned around and nodded at Finn, who was gaping at her.

"Come on," she said, "let's go."

Amelia went to go after her, but Maci pulled her back. She'd seen the look on Sydney's face, and she wanted no part of whatever the girl was planning to do next.

"Come on, Amelia, let's go," Maci hissed. "Please."

Amelia turned to give Maci an icy stare. "She can't talk to me like that," she said. "Who does she think she is?"

"Just drop it, Amelia," said Maci. "She's not worth it."

"She's not, but I'm not going to let her get away with this." Amelia gave Maci a smile that the girl didn't like. "Wait, I have an idea."

Flinging her hair over her shoulder, Amelia headed for Jeremy. Maci shook her head and, for the first time ever, didn't follow her.

Sydney and Finn headed outside to their usual spot by the fence and sat down on the grass.

"That side of you always surprises me," commented Finn. "You're scary. I hope you never get mad at me."

"I was just sticking up for myself."

"I know, and that's a good thing. But you sounded so mean."

Sydney watched Finn pick up a blade of grass and try to blow on it to make it whistle. After five tries, he managed to get a sound out of it.

"So, what are you doing this weekend?" she asked, leaning back on her hands. "I have to help Mom in the yard."

"Dad and I are going to the park to barbecue while the weather's still good," replied Finn, tossing the blade of grass.

"Sounds fun."

"Yeah, I guess."

"What's wrong?" asked Sydney. "You don't want to go?"

He shrugged. "I don't mind the cooking and eating part. It's the conversation I'm not looking forward to."

"I don't understand."

"We're going to talk about my mother."

"Oh. Why?"

Finn pulled his legs in to sit cross-legged. "Dad wants to terminate her parental rights."

"Wow, that's big."

"Yeah."

"Why does he want to do that?"

Finn sighed. "Every visit I have with her is terrible. She is either yelling at me or telling me I'm headed to hell for being gay."

"Oh, no."

"I mean, she's my mother, right? She should be supportive." He glanced away. "I mean, who tells their kid that? How is that loving?"

"I think she believes she's saving your soul," replied Sydney. "In her eyes, it's wrong to be gay."

"Why can't she see things through my eyes once in a while? I mean, geez, doesn't she understand how much it hurts when she says that?"

Finn fell back in the grass, and Sydney rolled on her side next to him, propping her head up on her hand.

"I'm sorry," she said. "I wish there was something I could do."

Finn gave her a little smile. "You do a lot by just listening."

"And sharing my pudding?"

"Yeah, that too," he said with a grin. "So, how are things with your dad?"

"He came over to see Mom the other day."

"Why?"

"He wanted to clear things up with her," said Sydney. "He also talked to me."

"I thought he wasn't supposed to see you at home?"

"Mom let him," replied Sydney.

"Oh. So how did it go?"

"He apologized."

"That's big."

"Maybe."

Finn sat up. "What does that mean?"

"I don't believe him," Sydney replied flatly. "I think it's a game to get on my good side so he doesn't have to have supervised visitation anymore."

"What does your mom think?"

Sydney shrugged. "I don't know."

"You haven't talked to her about this?"

"Not lately."

"Why?"

Sydney sat up and crossed her legs, leaning forward. "I don't want to deal with this," she replied. "I mean, I just want a normal life."

Finn laughed. "What's a normal life?"

"I don't know . . . maybe a mother and father who live together in harmony?"

"Not many people have that."

"I know."

"As a matter of fact, I don't know anyone who has that. I mean, who lives in harmony all the time?" Finn shook his head. "Maybe in giizhig."

A smile broke across Sydney's face. "Where did you learn the Ojibwa word for heaven?"

Finn smiled back. "I've made it a point to learn some Ojibwa words."

"Why?"

"Just in case you cuss at me in Ojibwa," he answered with a laugh. "I want to know what I'm being called."

Sydney grinned. "Just so you don't use any bad words in my direction."

"Deal."

The bell rang, and they got up and started heading inside. Finn took her hand and smiled as he gave it a kiss.

"I am grateful for you, my friend," he said with a smile. "I'm so glad you moved here last spring."

"I didn't want to move," she admitted, holding his hand tight in hers. "But now I see it was the best thing."

"Because you met me?" he asked with a twinkle in his eye.

"That too," she replied, grinning back. "You make me a better person."

"That's corny."

"Yup, it is. But it's true. You helped me see some truths about myself."

"Have you forgiven yourself for the way you treated that girl on the reservation?"

Sydney shook her head. "It's hard to do that when that person inside of me keeps rearing her ugly head."

Finn nodded, and they were silent for a moment. Sydney turned to glance at him.

"Finn, I really like you. I wish you weren't . . . well . . . I mean . . ."

He nodded. "I love you, Sydney. You're my best friend, my oasis in the desert, the shim to my sham, the ice cream to my cone. But I can't change who I am."

"I would never ask you to do that," she said quickly. "But the person who gets to be with you will be very lucky."

His grin lit up his face. "I feel the same about you," he said.

She held his hand up to her cheek. "Best friends?" she whispered.

He nodded.

"I can handle that," she said.

Just then a group of boys bumped into them on purpose, almost knocking Sydney over. She righted herself and glared at the blond-haired one.

"Jeremy . . . you're a clod."

Jeremy laughed and gave her a cold stare. "A clod? What does that even mean? Who uses words like that?"

"Someone with a vocabulary," replied Finn, grabbing Sydney's arm and moving her toward the back door of the school.

"What's she doing with you anyway? Doesn't she know you're queer?" Jeremy shot back.

When Finn bristled and started to slow down, Sydney urged him forward.

"Keep going, keep going," she muttered. "He's not worth it."

"No, he's not worth it," Finn answered loudly, glaring over at Jeremy.

Jeremy's friends laughed, and Jeremy gritted his teeth as his eyes narrowed. He reached over to grab Finn as his fist flew through the air and connected with someone's cheek.

The problem was it wasn't Finn's.

A Punch
to the Face

Sydney blinked several times as she lay on the ground. She had seen what was about to happen and pulled Finn away just in time, which put her in the line of fire.

Finn dropped down beside her as a group of kids gathered around them. Someone ran to get a teacher as Jeremy stood there, stunned, staring down at Sydney.

"I didn't mean to hit her! She got in the way. It was her fault." Jeremy frantically glanced at the kids around him as the teacher ran up.

The teacher took one look at Sydney, Jeremy, and Finn and then reached down to help Sydney up. "Jeremy Nickerson, head straight to the office. I will meet you there," he said coldly.

"How do you know *I* did this?" Jeremy blurted out.

The teacher glanced at Finn and snorted. "You've got to be kidding, right?" He shook his head. "I believe this will result in a suspension."

"But I have a game on Friday."

"Not anymore, you don't," replied the teacher. "I doubt you will be playing at all this year. Hitting someone, let alone a woman, is against school policy."

"But I didn't mean to hit her!" blustered Jeremy. "She got in the way."

"But you meant to hit someone, didn't you?" asked the teacher. "This is not the first time either."

"No, no . . . I am all right," whispered Sydney, holding her cheek now. She was shaken and a little wobbly on her feet, and it took both Finn and the teacher to get her into the building. They headed straight for the nurse's office.

"I'm okay," she said again, trying to pull away. "Please . . ."

Finn shook his head. "He hit you hard, Syd. You need to be looked at." He leaned down to catch her eyes.

"Why did you do that?" he whispered. "Now look at you. You have a gigantic bruise. I could have handled him."

Sydney shook her head but stopped when it made her dizzy. "Best friends forever," she whispered back.

Finn shook his head as he cursed loudly.

The teacher frowned and pointed down the hall as they reached the nurse's office. "Finn, go to class."

"No way! She took that hit for me. I'm not just going to leave her."

The teacher opened his mouth to retort but saw the distress in Finn's eyes as the boy tried not to cry. He sighed. "It's going to be okay," he said, "I have her. I will call her mother, and she's probably going home now. Go to class."

Finn stared into the teacher's eyes and then nodded. "Okay then." He glanced down at Sydney, his eyes filling with tears. "I'll call you later, okay?"

Sydney gave him a little smile. He straightened up, nodding curtly. Sydney glanced up to catch the look in his eyes, and she frowned.

"No, Finn. It stops here."

"He—"

"Two wrongs don't make a right."

"But he—"

"No, Finn. Please. Then all this will have been for nothing."

So much anger flashed across Finn's face that the teacher took a step back.

"We are better than that," Sydney reminded Finn, and he gritted his teeth and shook his head. They stared at each other for a moment, and then Finn sighed.

"Yes, we are," he admitted, and reluctantly turned and headed down the hall.

The nurse looked at Sydney while the teacher called her mother. Twenty minutes later, her mother ran into the room to see Sydney holding an ice pack to her cheek.

"Are you all right?" she asked, kneeling beside her daughter. "Who did this to you? What happened?"

"Like Mr. Sampson told you on the phone, she got in the middle of a fight and was hit by accident," replied the nurse. "I don't believe she has any broken bones, but she will have the bruise for quite a while. You can take her home for the day. Just call us tomorrow if she still isn't feeling well."

"I think she should go to the doctor," replied her mother, watching her daughter unsteadily get up off the chair.

"Mom, I'm fine," said Sydney, making her voice stronger than she felt. "I just want to go home."

Her mother nodded, and she and Sydney walked out of the nurse's office and headed down the hall toward her locker. As they passed the principal's office, they could hear voices, and Sydney recognized Jeremy's voice among two others.

"This is it, Jeremy," she heard the principal say. "I can no longer tolerate your behavior."

"You can kiss Friday's game goodbye," added the coach.

Sydney stopped, and holding up a finger to tell her mother to wait, she stepped into the office. The principal, the coach, and Jeremy stared at her.

"I'm sorry to interrupt, but this is not Jeremy's fault," she said, and Jeremy's eyes flew wide open. "He was having an argument with my friend, and it got out of hand," she added. "He never meant to hit me."

She turned to give Jeremy a small nod. "I forgive you. I'm going to be okay. We need to just move on. Finn has."

For a moment, no one in the office spoke. Then the principal cleared his throat and nodded.

"That's an amazing thing to say, Sydney," he said. "That's very gracious of you. But Jeremy has been in trouble before." He sighed and crossed his arms. "I will take care of this situation now. You go home and rest."

"But, sir, isn't he needed on the football team?" asked Sydney.

"His behavior is unbecoming of a player, Sydney," said Coach Ray, who was sitting to the left of the principal. "I will be removing him from the game this week."

"Please don't do this because of me," Sydney said, frantically glancing from Jeremy to the principal to the coach. "You don't understand. Everyone in school will hate me if that happens."

"Sydney," said her mother, "I think we need to let the principal decide what he is going to do now. You need to go home and rest."

"It's not just one thing, Sydney," replied the principal. "He has a long list of issues."

"Don't we all?" said Sydney, glancing around again to everyone in the room.

The room went silent for a moment as Sydney searched her mind for a solution.

"Look, what if he can make it up to me?" she asked the principal. "And prove he's worth being on the football team?"

The principal shook his head but was interrupted by the coach.

"What are you thinking?" the coach asked.

Sydney turned to the principal. "My father is gone, and it's just Mom and me," she said.

"Sydney . . . ," interjected her mother, but Sydney shook her head.

"We could use some help around the house sometimes. You know, mowing, fixing stuff, things like that. If Jeremy is handy with things like that, he can come over once a week to help us out."

"So, he would be working his behavior off, so to speak?" asked the principal. "That's an interesting idea."

"Wait," said Jeremy. "I don't think—"

"We could use the help," Sydney said, glaring at him. "And frankly, you need to prove to everyone you're worth more than a backward glance before they throw you and your football career down the river."

"Sydney!" her mother said, frowning. "That was not very nice."

Sydney pulled the ice pack from her face and stared at her mother. "This could have been Finn. And all because he is trying to live his best life." She shrugged. "I don't know if Jeremy's worth it, but I do think he's probably gotten to the point where this might be his last chance."

Sydney glanced down at Jeremy in the chair. "It's really up to him. He's the one with something to prove to everyone."

All eyes turned to Jeremy now as he mulled over what had been said around him. Why was this girl standing up for him? She was nothing in his eyes, except a friend to that weirdo, Finn. Finn was nothing too. Neither of them mattered.

He sighed. What choice did he have? It was either do what the girl wanted or lose his football career. Football was all he had, as he wasn't known to be "academically inclined," as his parents put it.

"How long will I be doing this?" he grumbled to no one in particular. The principal sighed angrily and leaned forward to respond. This boy wouldn't know a lifeline if it bit him.

"As long as I say," answered Sydney.

Jeremy turned to look at her and winced. Her bruise had quickly darkened against her Native skin and turned an ugly purple color.

"Why are you doing this?" he asked, and became uncomfortable with the way she held his gaze. It was as if she could see right inside him somehow, and he didn't like it.

She shrugged. "We need the help, and apparently so do you."

He bit the inside of his lip, considering all his options. None of them looked good, but maybe he could play this game until things cooled down.

"Fine," he muttered. "I'll go over once a week and help them out with stuff."

Sydney's mouth twitched into a small smile, and the principal frowned. He addressed Sydney's mother now.

"Are you all right with this?" he asked, still unsure.

She nodded. "Under certain stipulations," she said, sighing, catching Sydney's pleading look.

"I decide what day you will come over, and you will be told what to do when you arrive. It will be the same day each week. You'll be there for two hours, and you will not be there unless I am there. You will be respectful to both my daughter and myself. There's no swearing in my house. There is no payment for any of the work. You come over, get instructions from me, and get the work done. Then you go home. Do I make myself clear?"

Jeremy nodded.

"And," added the principal, "if this doesn't work out for any reason, you will come back and see me and Coach again to decide your future at this school. Do you understand all this?"

"Yes."

"I believe you owe Sydney a big thank-you," said the coach. "I was considering throwing you off the team."

"Thanks," he mumbled, refusing to look at her this time.

"I will talk with Jeremy's parents about this arrangement," said the principal. "Miss Coffman, you have a very intelligent daughter."

"Thank you," she replied, as she started to usher her daughter out of the office.

Jeremy looked up to see Sydney place the ice pack back over her cheek. She paused for a moment and then turned around, giving him a nod.

"See you soon," she said, and he watched her walk away.

Jeremy shook his head as the principal shut the door behind them. He turned around to face the desk and sighed, dropping his face in his hand.

The next couple of weeks were going to suck.

Things Are Changing

F inn was sitting on the front step with Sydney as they watched Jeremy mow the lawn.

"He doesn't look too happy," commented Finn, noticing the scowl on Jeremy's face. "How long is he going to have to come over here?"

"Until I decide," replied Sydney, taking a sip of lemonade. "And I don't care if he doesn't like it. I don't have to do it. I hate mowing."

Finn grinned. "Ah, it's not too bad. It's trimming the bushes I hate."

"Maybe I should send him over to help you out."

Finn shook his head. "Don't do that. The guy already hates me."

"Well, he's not too fond of me either," she said.

"The whole school knows what happened," said Finn.

"I don't care."

"You really don't, do you?"

Sydney shrugged. "No one likes me anyway. I have nothing to prove to anyone. They can think what they like."

"That's not true."

"What do you mean?"

"I like you."

Sydney grinned. "I thank Gitchie Manitou every day for that."

"Gitchie who?"

"You know very well who I'm talking about. Just because you don't believe in him doesn't mean you don't know who he is."

"I never said I didn't believe in him. I just said I wasn't sure about all that stuff."

"Well, if it wasn't for him and you, I would have no one to talk to," said Sydney, leaning back on the step.

"You talk to him?" asked Finn.

"Every day, just like I talk to you."

"Huh. Does he answer?"

Sydney thought about that for a moment. "He does. But it's not always in words. Sometimes it's the actions of another person, or a thought flitting through my mind."

"That's deep."

Sydney didn't respond. She closed her eyes and sighed. She could feel the sun beating down on her, making her perspire a little. There was no breeze at all, and her mind sank into itself for a moment.

"Sydney?"

"Hmm?"

"Can we go inside? It's hot out here."

"Sure."

She opened her eyes and got up. Finn followed her into the house as Jeremy made his way to the backyard.

As they walked into the kitchen, Sydney glanced out the window.

"Do you think I should go give him a drink?" she asked, seeing how sweaty Jeremy was. "He's probably thirsty."

"Do you really care if he is?" asked Finn, frowning.

Sydney shrugged.

"I guess so then. I'm going to go use the bathroom."

Sydney nodded and watched Finn disappear around the corner. Then she got a glass out of the cupboard and filled it with lemonade. She stepped out the back door and waited for Jeremy to turn the mower around and notice her. When he finally did, he glanced at her and then ignored her, mowing right past her.

She sighed and called out his name. At first, he pretended not to hear her, but when he turned the mower around again and saw the look in her eyes, he thought better of it.

He shut the mower off and wiped his forehead.

"What?" he asked impatiently.

Put off by his tone, she almost turned to go back inside. He saw that hesitation and sighed, reluctantly walking over to her.

He stopped a couple of feet away, and they stared at each other for a moment before she spoke.

"I thought you might be thirsty," she said, thrusting the glass out in front of her.

Surprise filled his eyes as he reached out to take it from her. He quickly downed the drink and then wiped his mouth.

"Your two hours are up," she said. "You can go now. I'll finish the mowing."

He looked down at the glass and then over at the mower.

"Fine," he said, and gave her back the glass before he walked away.

Sighing, she walked over and set the glass down by the back door before heading over to the lawn mower.

She pulled the cord a couple of times but couldn't get it started. Frowning in frustration, she wondered if Finn was out of the bathroom yet. She glanced at the house but could see no sign of him. She reached down and tried to get the mower started again.

Finn was, in fact, watching from the bathroom window. When he saw she was having trouble, he turned to go help her, but a movement out of the corner of his eye caught his attention.

Sydney looked up to see Jeremy striding across the lawn. When he reached her, he gently pushed her out of the way and reached down to pull the lawn mower cord. The machine roared to life.

"I'll finish," said Jeremy curtly, and he pushed the lawn mower away from her.

Her eyes narrowed as she watched him for a moment. Then she turned to go back in the house.

Finn also turned from the bathroom window. He saw the frustration in Sydney's eyes, and he didn't blame her. But there was something else there, too, and he wondered about it.

It was sorrow, and he couldn't for the life of him figure out why.

He met her in the kitchen a moment later. He watched her wash the glass and put it away. Then she wiped down the already-clean counters and hung up the washcloth over the faucet.

"You okay?" he asked.

"Yeah."

"Did Jeremy give you a hard time?"

Sydney shook her head.

"So, then what's up?" asked Finn.

"I don't understand the question."

"Yes, you do."

Sydney headed into the living room, and Finn followed behind her. Sydney sat cross-legged on the couch, and Finn sat down and leaned back against it.

"He came back to finish the mowing," she said, thoughtful now.

"So? He should have. He was almost done."

"I feel bad for him," she said.

Finn frowned. "You've got to be kidding. Why?"

"He looks lonely."

"What? Where did you get that?"

"Something in his eyes."

"Sydney, he hangs around with a whole pack of football players."

She nodded. "Well, I used to hang out with these girls from my old school. We hung out at school but hardly did as much stuff outside of school as I would have liked." She sighed and looked away. "I was kind of lonely, and I recognize that in other people now."

"Why didn't you guys hang out a lot?"

"Jayden had dance; Bree was busy with karate . . . It seemed like everyone was too busy with stuff."

"Oh."

"And things with my dad . . . well, they weren't going so well."

"I'm sorry."

"It's okay, but I was just thinking about Jeremy. Like I said, he seems kind of lonely."

"Well, I don't see that," said Finn, shaking his head. "Anyway, why do you care?"

Sydney shrugged. "Something about his eyes makes me sad."

"I can't believe you're giving him any thought at all."

"It was just a random thought."

"You are too nice to everybody."

Sydney laughed. "I can't think of the last person who told me that."

"Well, you are. You stand up for me all the time." Finn looked over at her. "I don't know what I would do without you."

Sydney smiled. "You never have to worry about it. You're not getting rid of me ever."

"Ever, huh? Hmm . . . won't your husband eventually wonder why I'm hanging around so much?" teased Finn. "He's going to want me to go home."

"You can live with us."

"Heck no. That would not work out at all," he replied, giving her a grimace.

She laughed and got up, then reached down to pull him up too. "Come on, let's get our homework done."

"Bossy," replied Finn as she pulled him back into the kitchen to sit at the table.

They opened their books and started working. A few minutes later, Finn glanced up to ask her about his math, and he caught her looking through the kitchen window at Jeremy, who was just finishing up the back lawn.

Finn opened his mouth and then closed it again, watching a wave of emotions wash across Sydney's face. Finn stared at her for a moment and then looked back down at his book, seeing nothing. He swallowed hard.

He hoped things weren't headed in the direction he thought they might be going. If they were, his best friend was headed for a deep well of hurt.

Forgotten Friend

A couple of weeks went by, and Finn forgot all about the conversation until he saw Sydney and Jeremy in the hall talking.

He put his books in his locker and hesitated before making the decision to approach her.

"Yeah, my mom appreciates all the work you're doing for us," said Sydney, and Jeremy nodded.

"I think she's going to have you scrub the patio off next time you come," Sydney continued. "It's really dirty. I washed down the chairs and table the other day, and they were a mess."

"Okay," replied Jeremy, shuffling his books to the other arm. He opened his mouth to say something and then glanced up and saw Finn approaching.

"See you," Jeremy said with a frown, and he turned and walked away.

Sydney watched him for a moment and then smiled as she saw Finn approach.

"Hi," she said with a smile. "Ready to go to math?"

"Who's ever ready for math?"

Sydney laughed and linked arms with him as they started down the hall.

"So, what were you two talking about?" asked Finn, glancing at her.

"Nothing, really. I was just telling him how much we appreciate his help around the house."

"Why? He's working off punching you in the face."

"Actually, he was aiming for you," said Sydney with a grin.

"Well, he would never work that off at my house," replied Finn. "He hates my guts. I can't understand why you're so nice to him after what he did."

"It pays to be kind."

"Not always," replied Finn.

"Well, this time it does. Has he bothered you since the incident?"

Finn shook his head. "Not so far. Maybe he's taking a break."

"Then maybe something good came out of all this."

"Did it? And what would that be?"

"Finn . . ."

"You look beautiful today," he said, trying to change the subject.

"What? Oh, thanks. I went shopping."

Finn looked her over and smiled. The sapphire-blue pants went well with the deep red flowy shirt she was wearing. Her white moccasins brought the outfit together.

"You could use a makeover," said Sydney, eyeing the green shirt he had already worn twice that week. "Don't you have any other shirts?" she asked.

"Yeah."

"Why don't you wear them?"

Finn shrugged. "I don't know. I don't really care what I look like. No one pays attention to me anyway."

"Well, I do, and you need some help. At least comb your hair."

"Why all this sudden interest in my attire and grooming habits?" he asked.

"How are you going to catch anyone's eye looking like that? Do you think you're the only gay person in the school?"

Finn nodded. "It seems that way."

"I think you're wrong."

"Why, what did you hear?" he asked, eager now.

"It makes sense that in a school population of this size, there is more than one gay person in the school."

Finn's disappointment was obvious, and Sydney gave him a smile.

"Are you looking for someone to play dress-up with?" she asked, and he frowned.

"What?"

"You know, then you can wear a dress."

"Wear a dress?" repeated Finn a little too loudly. People glanced over at them, and he grimaced, looking down at the ground.

They stopped just to the left of the door of the math class, and Sydney turned to look at him.

"Did I say something wrong?" she asked when she saw his expression.

"Sydney, not all gay people are transgender," he hissed under his breath.

"Oh. But I thought . . ."

"It's a misconception," he said, upset now. "A common one, by the way."

Sydney caught the look in his eyes and hung her head. "Finn, I am so sorry. I should just shut up about things I don't know anything about. Please forgive me."

Finn saw the expression on her face and sighed. "Come on, let's go. It's fine. I'm over it. Let's go learn something."

"I think I already did," whispered Sydney, and Finn nodded as they entered the classroom.

As the day dragged on, Sydney thought about their conversation. Before the last class, she met him at his locker.

"Wanna walk home together?" she asked. "I want to talk to you about something."

Finn had been driven home after school by his father since school began in the fall, but he nodded now. He pulled his phone out of his pocket as they exited the school, and talked with his father. After a moment, he hung up.

"Dad said to call him if we have any problems," said Finn. "He will come get us right away."

"Okay."

They met an hour later and headed out the side door.

"So, what did you want to talk about?" asked Finn.

"Jeremy."

Finn rolled his eyes. "Oh."

Sydney laughed and took his arm as they walked. "Just listen, will you?"

"I guess," Finn grumbled.

"Why do you think Jeremy is so tough on you?" asked Sydney. "Why won't he leave you alone?"

"Who knows? He hates me."

"But why? He hardly knows you," answered Sydney. "I think if we can figure out the reason, then maybe we can get him to stop for good."

Finn laughed. "No way. He doesn't care what either of us thinks."

"How long have you known him?"

"Since grade school."

"Has he always bothered you?" asked Sydney.

"No."

"When did it start?"

"The beginning of middle school, I guess."

Sydney thought about that for a moment. "I wonder why it started then?"

"I was beginning to realize that I was not into girls like some of my friends were. I think eventually my friends started to drift away because they could see what I was before I admitted it to myself."

"You had friends?" Sydney teased, and Finn shook his head.

"Not funny, Syd. I had a lot of friends once upon a time."

Sydney's smile left her face, as she could see the sadness in his eyes. "Sorry, I was just teasing."

"Yeah."

"So, then what?" she asked, gently prodding him to continue.

"As soon as I realized I was gay, I also realized that the guys didn't want to hang around me anymore."

"Why?" asked Sydney.

Finn shrugged. "Maybe they thought if they did, people would think they were gay. They could see I was getting picked on. They probably didn't want that for themselves."

Sydney mulled that over for a while before turning back to him. "Gotaaji."

"What?" he asked.

"It's fear," said Sydney. "The whole thing stems from fear."

"They're afraid of me?" asked Finn. He laughed. "I don't think so."

"No, they're afraid of the stigma of being gay," said Sydney. "And I bet some of them are."

"Are what?"

"Gay."

"What are you talking about?" asked Finn. "Who's gay?"

"Those people who see you're being bullied and don't want the same thing to happen to them," answered Sydney.

"So, what you're saying is that some people are afraid to be anywhere near me because then people will think they are gay, and then they will get harassed too?"

"Yup."

"But they have a choice," he pointed out. "They don't have to come near me. They could stay away. But they make the choice to harass me."

"It's the wrong choice," admitted Sydney. "But because they harass you, no one would ever think they were gay. It's their secret."

Sydney was quiet again for a moment and then asked, "Who did you used to hang around with?"

"What?"

"Who were your friends before?" she asked.

He shrugged. "No one. It doesn't matter."

"Of course it does," replied Sydney. "Name one. Do I know them?"

No . . . yes. I guess so. One of them anyway."

"Who is it?"

"I don't want to talk about this anymore."

"Finn, I'm just trying to help. Name someone. Maybe I can go talk to them."

"It won't help."

"How do you know that?"

"I just do!"

"Don't get upset," replied Sydney. "I'm just trying to help you."

"Well, you can't do anything, okay? Just let it be."

"Come on, just give me one name."

Finn shook his head. "I don't want to. Leave it alone."

"I don't understand why," said Sydney. "Don't you want things to get better?"

"They won't."

"How do you know that?"

"Because it's Jeremy, okay? Jeremy used to be my best friend."

Trying to Help

Sydney was waiting on the front steps when Jeremy came walking up the driveway. His mother had dropped him off on the way to the store and promised she would be back in exactly two hours.

His hair was a little too long, Sydney noticed. It was starting to curl up on the ends due to the heat. He was getting a bleached-blond surfer look to him now. He wasn't big and burly like the other football players. As the quarterback, he was leaner and tightly muscled. And she had seen him run. He was fast.

But it was his eyes that captivated her. There was so much in those eyes . . .

Sydney gathered herself together as he approached. "I want to talk to you," she said, patting the step next to her.

"I'm here to work."

"Yeah, but this will only take a minute."

Jeremy sighed as he stopped in front of her and crossed his arms.

"Now what do you want?" he asked.

"Sit down."

"Nope. I don't plan to stand here long."

Sydney took a deep breath and then caught his gaze. "What happened between you and Finn?"

Jeremy was taken aback by the question and didn't answer it right away. He dropped his arms to his sides. "Nothing."

"You were friends once," pointed out Sydney.

"Yeah, so? People move on. Is that it? I have work to do."

He started to walk away toward the back of the house, with Sydney trailing behind him. Sydney's mother, Dakotah, saw him through the kitchen window and stepped out the back door.

"I need the patio cleaned," she said. "I bought some special stuff to do it with. It's over here."

Jeremy followed her over to the other side of the large patio and looked at what she'd bought. With a nod, she glanced at Sydney and walked back into the house.

"I would like a better answer than that," said Sydney.

"What?"

"About Finn."

"I have nothing more to say about it," he replied, getting busy on the patio.

"That's sad." She turned to go. "I can see having friends doesn't mean anything to you."

"Excuse me?"

"You heard me."

Jeremy watched Sydney take a step toward him.

"You were Finn's best friend," she said, putting her hands on her hips. "Now you want nothing to do with him. Why is that, Jeremy? Is it because you're hanging around all those football guys now, acting like you're some big thing? You and I know you're not."

She took another step toward him. His eyes narrowed and he went to speak, but she cut him off.

"Who'd you replace Finn with, huh? Will, the loudmouth class cutup, or was it Josh, who's flunking math?" Sydney turned to go. "You sure picked some winners."

She was surprised when Jeremy reached out to grab her arm. It jerked her to a halt, and she pulled out of his grasp and turned around to face him.

"Don't ever touch me again," she spat out angrily. "You have no right to put your hands on me or anyone else." She turned back around and started walking away, saying, "Save it for the field."

"Then stop talking to me!" he snapped out.

Sydney whipped around. "This is my house, and I will talk to whomever I want to." The smile she gave him did not reach her eyes as she added, "What are you going to do about it?" She waved a hand dismissively. "Get back to work."

"Sydney, is there an issue?" asked her mother, concerned, coming out the back door. "I could hear yelling all the way from the bedroom."

Sydney glanced over at Jeremy, who remained silent. He knew he was in trouble again. He had broken one of the rules Dakotah had given him by being disrespectful to Sydney. It wouldn't matter that she started the whole thing. He dropped his head and sighed. He was off the team for sure this time.

Sydney stared over at Jeremy for a moment before giving her mother a reassuring smile.

"No, we were just goofing around," she said. "I'm going in to do my homework now."

Sydney gently pushed her mother into the house ahead of her, giving a stunned Jeremy a backward glance. Her eyes narrowed, and then dismissively, she pulled the door shut behind them.

For a moment, Jeremy didn't move. She'd saved him again. Even though she started it all, he had grabbed her, and she could have told her mother. He didn't understand what was going on with her. She couldn't possibly like him, so why had she covered for him?

Jeremy didn't see Sydney again until he was about to leave. He knocked on the door, and she opened it, eyeing him.

"I'm done," he said, and she nodded.

"Fine," she replied. "I'll let Mom know."

She went to close the door but stopped when he spoke.

"I'm sorry I grabbed you. You made me mad though."

"You made me mad too," she replied. "You hurt my friend Finn. And by the way, being mad is no reason to put your hands on someone," Sydney pointed out.

"Sorry," he said again. When she nodded, he added, "I'm sorry you got hit. I've never hit a girl before."

"I guess that makes me special then," she said sarcastically, and he shrugged.

"Yes. I mean . . . um . . . you are the only one, so, anyway . . . bye."

Jeremy walked quickly down the steps and onto the driveway as his mother showed up. Sydney watched him leave, and then she closed the door.

When she turned around, her mother was there.

Dakotah crossed her arms. "So, do you want to tell me what's going on between you and Jeremy?"

The Wrong Move

Finn was coming out of his science class when Jeremy approached him. He was alone, and Finn tensed when he saw him.

"I want to talk to you," said Jeremy, falling in step next to Finn, who was headed to his next class.

"Why? What would you possibly have to say that I would care to hear?" asked Finn, staring at him.

"You need to keep your 'girlfriend' away from me," said Jeremy. "And I use that word loosely. We both know what you are."

"What are you talking about?"

"I went over there yesterday to work at her house, and she cornered me and started yelling at me," replied Jeremy.

"Why?"

"Something about us once being friends and why we aren't friends anymore."

"What?"

"Yeah, you must have told her about us being friends when we were little." Jeremy snickered. "You know why we don't hang out anymore. I don't have to explain myself to her."

"No, you don't," agreed Finn. "I had no idea she was going to talk to you about this. I told her that in confidence." Finn gritted his teeth and added, "I'll have a talk with her."

"You do that."

"I'd say I'm sorry this happened," said Finn, "but I couldn't care less what happens to you now after what you've done to me in the past several years." He sighed, adding, "Both people I thought were my friends betrayed my confidence. I guess I'm not a good judge of character."

Jeremy stopped in the middle of the hall, other students brushing past him. "What does that mean?"

Finn stopped too. "You and I both know the lies and rumors you've spread about me. I know it was you." He took a step toward Jeremy and stared him down. "You were my best friend, Jeremy. We knew everything about each other. When you figured out I was gay, you wouldn't have anything to do with me. You took everything I told you in confidence and spread it around school, adding your own little twist on things to make it more interesting." Finn's voice was getting loud now, but he didn't notice. "None of my friends would speak to me anymore, and all because of the lies you made up about me."

"You deserve everything you got," snapped Jeremy, taking a step toward Finn. "You hung out with me knowing when people found out about you, they would think I was gay too."

"They don't think you're gay, Jeremy. They think you're stupid," Finn ground out. "Maybe I should stoop down to your level and start telling people what I know about you."

Jeremy laughed. "There's nothing to tell."

Finn's eyebrows went up, and a smile spread across his face. "Really? We'll see about that." He turned to go.

Only then did he notice the little crowd around them watching the scene unfold. He pushed through them and started walking down the hall.

A moment later, Jeremy's hand grabbed his shoulder and swung him around. The crowd backed up as Finn pulled free to face him.

The two stared at each other as two teachers ran down the hall toward them. Seeing them, Jeremy backed away, shoving his hands in his pants pockets and changing the expression on his face to one of calmness.

"Finn, are you okay?" asked Mr. Rodamacher, reaching out to turn Finn around to face him.

"Hey, why are you asking *him* if he's okay?" asked Jeremy. "What about me?"

The teacher shot him a look. "Really?"

The other teacher got to Finn as Mr. Rodamacher let him go.

"What's going on here?" she asked, and they both turned to look at Jeremy, who remained silently indignant.

Finn took a look at the teachers and then at Jeremy. He straightened his backpack and turned to go.

"Who's the loser now?" he said, glancing at Jeremy. He snickered and then walked away as the teachers surrounded Jeremy.

Sydney was in the middle of the hall when she noticed what was going on. She caught Jeremy's icy glare at Finn as Finn strode away from the crowd.

"What's happening?" she asked Finn as he approached her.

He didn't respond, pushing past her and heading down the hall.

"Finn?"

Sydney ran to catch up with him, and he shook his head.

"Stay away from me," he sneered. "This is your fault. You stuck your nose in where it didn't belong and made things worse. Just leave me alone."

"I don't know what you're talking about."

Finn stopped and turned to face her. He took a step toward her, and seeing the look in his eye, she automatically took a step back.

"You confronted Jeremy about he and I not being friends," said Finn, pointing his finger at her. "What was that supposed to accomplish?"

"I was just trying to help," replied Sydney. "I thought I could make him understand . . ."

"Well, you didn't. And he confronted me about it, and now he's in more trouble. You did nothing but make things worse for everyone."

"I'm sorry . . ."

Finn shook his head. "He said you yelled at him." He took another step toward her. "Did the old Sydney come out again?" he asked sarcastically. "You can't bully a bully, you know."

He turned to go. "I told you about Jeremy in private, Sydney. It's obvious I can't trust you." He shook his head and pulled his backpack closer to him. "I need a break from us, Sydney. You are not the friend I thought I had."

Sydney watched him walk down the hall until he turned the corner. Tears welled up in her eyes, and she dropped her head. She gathered her books close to her chest and turned around, heading down the hall.

Painful Day

As Sydney was sitting down to dinner, there was a knock at the door. Her mother glanced at her and set the pot roast down on the dining table. Sydney shook her head, and her mother went to answer the door.

It was the postman with a registered letter. Sydney's mother, Dakotah, signed for it and then shut the door.

"What is it, Mom?" asked Sydney, helping herself to some food. "It's pretty late for the postman to be still delivering mail, isn't it?"

Dakotah frowned as she examined the letter and then carefully opened it up. It was from her ex-husband. He had written a brief message to her and then included some court papers he had filed recently. Dakotah sat down at the table, reading them.

"It seems your father wants to be sure I know he has asked the court to have the supervised visitation decision reversed," said Dakotah. "He sent me some paperwork here, but I'm guessing I'll get my own batch from the court in the mail soon."

Sydney put down her fork and gazed at her mother. "I don't want that," she said. "I like things the way they are."

Dakotah nodded. "Me too," she replied. "But he has been going to counseling and doing whatever the court has asked him to do."

"It's too soon, Mom."

"I think so too."

"So, what are we going to do?"

Dakotah shrugged. "Go back to court, I guess."

"Will I have to go?"

"I would think you would want a say in your own life. The only way to get that is to go."

"I guess."

They were silent for a bit as they ate, each in their own thoughts. Sydney was still upset about her fight with Finn, and Dakotah was worried about the fight she was about to have with Sydney's father.

"Sydney, are you all right?" asked her mother, eyeing her from across the dinner table.

"Yeah, I'm fine," she replied.

"Is Jeremy bothering you?"

Sydney considered that question and then replied, "No."

"I don't know what's going on with you two, but it sounds like it could become a problem," said her mother. "Just stay away from him."

Sydney didn't respond as she shoveled more potatoes into her mouth. Dakotah glanced at her and then shook her head, changing the subject.

"I thought we could go on vacation around Thanksgiving time," she said. "It seems silly to make a big dinner for just the two of us, and with no family around, I thought maybe it would be a good time to get away."

"What about Dad?"

Dakotah shrugged. "The court date is in January. You are under no obligation to see him outside of the supervised visitation, and I doubt they would let you do so anyway."

"Where do you want to go?"

Dakotah smiled. "I have four days off. I thought maybe we could decide on somewhere together."

"Okay."

"Someplace warm though," added her mother. "I want to lie in the sun and read a book."

"Florida?"

"Hmm . . . it's the tail end of hurricane season down there. Tell you what. Let's go ahead and plan on the Gulf side of Florida for a quiet vacation. We can rent a house and make our own meals. We'll watch the weather to make sure we can go."

"Is it warm in November?"

"It's warmer than it is here," replied her mother. "Around seventy-seven degrees, I think. At least warm enough for shorts."

"I don't know if you'll get a tan."

Dakotah laughed. "I don't need one. I just need a break from life."

Sydney smiled. "I think it sounds great. I could use one too."

Sydney thought about the trip as she got ready for bed. It would be nice to get away for a while.

As she pulled the covers up over her shoulders and turned over, she thought back to Jeremy and Finn. A sadness filled her eyes, and she wiped a tear away. She'd lost her only friend. She knew he was more than mad; he was hurt. She'd just been trying to help. That's what friends did for each other.

Telling herself to go to sleep now, she tried to settle down, but she became restless. She was starting to feel unwell but couldn't put her finger on what the issue was. Eventually exhaustion overtook her, and she drifted off into a troubled sleep.

The next morning, Sydney felt sluggish. She got up slowly, wondering what was wrong with her. Her abdomen hurt, and she wondered what she'd eaten to cause her to feel as though she was going to throw up.

She dressed in baggy sweatpants and a T-shirt before grabbing her backpack and heading into the kitchen. Her mother was already there, making herself lunch.

"Sydney, I will be late getting home tonight," Dakotah said. "I have a meeting after work for a special project."

"All right."

Dakotah glanced behind her and frowned. She put the knife down she was using to spread mayo on her sandwich and walked over to her daughter.

"Are you okay, honey?" she asked, concerned at the unusual paleness of Sydney's face. She put a hand on her daughter's forehead. "You have a fever," she announced, taking her daughter's bag off of her shoulder and setting it down on the floor. "You go right back to bed."

"Mom, no. I have a test today in science," protested Sydney. "My stomach hurts, but I think it must have been something I ate. Just give me some medicine, and I'll get going."

"Are you sure?" Dakotah asked, feeling pulled in two different directions. She was so busy at work, but Sydney didn't look well at all. "You can't go to school with a fever," she pointed out. "It's against school policy."

"I'm fine. I need to go to science class at least. I'll call you if I feel worse." Sydney reached down to pull her book bag off the floor and grimaced. She gave her mother a reassuring smile and headed toward the door.

"All right," sighed Dakotah, going against her better judgment. "Go get in the car, and I'll be there in a minute."

Dakotah heard the door shut as she reached for a cup and headed for the kitchen faucet for water. While she used the microwave to warm the water, she opened her own medicine bag from around her neck and pulled out some crushed peppermint leaves. When the water was hot, she poured it over the leaves, which she had put in a tea leaf strainer. Then she put the tea into a small thermos, grabbed her sandwich and lunch bag, and headed out the door.

"Here, take this," Sydney's mother said, handing her the thermos. "It's peppermint tea. It should make your stomach feel better. I hope this works. If not, call me right away, and I will come and get you."

Sydney nodded. "Dad used to make this tea for me when I was little," she said with a little smile.

They got in the car, and Sydney opened the thermos and took a sip. The drink was hot, but not too bad. She took another drink and closed her eyes as she swallowed it down.

Moments later, they were out in front of the school. Dakotah glanced at her daughter with growing concern.

"Sydney, I really think—"

"I'm fine. I'll be all right. Pick me up after school, okay?"

"You're not walking home with Finn?"

"Not today."

"Okay then. I hope you feel better soon."

Sydney got out of the car and headed for the front door of the school. She managed to get to her locker and deposit her book bag. Then she pulled out the stuff she needed for her first class and headed down the hall.

She passed a bathroom, then stopped and headed inside. She felt as if she was going to throw up. She quickly stepped into a stall, but other than a few coughs, nothing came up.

When she was sure nothing was going to happen, she stepped out of the stall and went over to wash her hands. Then she headed to class.

She found her seat and lowered herself down into it. She was not feeling herself but thought maybe it was stress. She opened her book as the teacher started the class, and tried to listen.

Jeremy was in the back of the room, watching her. Normally she smiled at him or gave him a little friendly wave, which he pointedly ignored, but not today. Today she looked as if she'd been run over by a truck.

He was mad at her. She'd stuck her nose in where it didn't belong, and now he was in trouble all over again for his confrontation with Finn in the hall the day before. He wanted to pull her aside and tell her to stay out of his business and that he would no longer be coming to her house for any more work. But that would have to wait until after class now.

The more time dragged on, the worse Sydney felt. She couldn't concentrate, and her abdomen was really starting to hurt now. The tea her mother had given her hadn't helped at all.

Forty-five minutes went by, and the bell was about to ring. Sydney gathered her stuff together and took deep breaths, trying to calm herself. When the bell rang, she stood up.

She instantly doubled over, groaning, and the kids around her frowned and snickered. The teacher came up and started talking to her, but she couldn't answer and couldn't move.

The teacher took one look at her face and said, "Let's get you to the nurse."

Sydney nodded and tried to walk but stopped because of the pain. Seconds later, she was gently picked up and carried down the hall.

She raised her head to look into Jeremy's eyes. She started to speak, and he shook his head. She stared at him for a moment and then sighed, laying her head against his shoulder, grimacing from the pain.

He could feel the heat radiating from her and knew she had a fever. He quickened his steps and got to the nurse's room before the teacher. He set her down in a chair and stepped back.

The nurse wasn't in the room but arrived a moment later. She took one look at Sydney and grabbed her thermometer to take her temp.

"It's high," the nurse said to the teacher, who had just arrived. "What happened?"

The teacher opened his mouth, but Jeremy talked for him.

"She came into the room looking sick," he said. "She didn't look good the whole time she was sitting there. Then when she stood up to leave, she almost collapsed. I grabbed her before she fell, and carried her here."

Both the nurse and teacher were surprised by the concern they saw in Jeremy's eyes.

The nurse nodded. "Okay, we'll take it from here. You can go back to class."

Jeremy nodded back and, with a last look at Sydney, turned to go.

"Thank you," said Sydney.

Jeremy glanced back at Sydney, who gave him a small smile. He gave her a curt nod and left.

About twenty minutes into his next class, Jeremy heard the ambulance siren screaming as it approached the school. He got up in the middle of class and looked out the window, and other students followed him. Minutes later, he caught his breath as Sydney was rolled out on a stretcher and put in the back of the ambulance. A moment later, it raced off.

The teacher got control of the class, and for the next half of the class, Jeremy sat in his chair, not paying attention or hearing a thing. All he could think of was Sydney being wheeled into the back of that ambulance and taken away.

The bell finally rang, and he walked quickly down the hall to Finn's locker. He'd pushed the kid every time he went by it, so he knew where it was.

Finn was there putting his books away when Jeremy approached. Jeremy pushed the locker closed with his hand.

"What the——" Finn started to say, and then he saw the look in Jeremy's eyes. "What's the matter with you?"

"They took Sydney away in an ambulance."

"What? When?"

"About twenty minutes ago."

"Why?"

"She was in pain and had a fever," replied Jeremy. "She didn't look good."

Finn bit off a swear word and then glanced at Jeremy. "I don't know what to do."

Jeremy nodded.

"I mean, they won't let me leave."

"I know."

"Do you think she's going to be okay?"

Jeremy shook his head. "I don't know."

"We have to go to class."

"Yes."

"Will you meet me after school? Maybe we can get in to see her."

Jeremy was silent for a moment and then stared at Finn. "We?"

"You want to see her, don't you?" asked Finn. "You're worried about her, otherwise you wouldn't have told me about her."

Jeremy sighed as he wrestled with his thoughts and feelings about Sydney and Finn. He could just walk away from all this. It was none of his business.

But the girl had gotten under his skin now. He didn't like her at all, but for some reason he was worried about her.

Finn watched with a frown as the emotions played over Jeremy's face. He didn't like what seemed to be happening between Sydney and Jeremy, but he couldn't do a thing to stop it.

Jeremy sighed, realizing the ship of blowing the situation off had long passed by without him even knowing it. He swallowed his anger and decided to give him chance, so he gave Finn a nod. "All right, fine. Meet me at the side door after school. I'll call my mom for a ride."

"What if they won't let us see her?" asked Finn, biting his lip.

"Then we wait until they do."

Finn nodded and turned to go. A moment later, he turned around. "Thanks, Jeremy."

Jeremy watched Finn walk down the hall and disappear into a room, and then he started walking the opposite way.

What was happening to him? He shook his head, trying to clear it. He didn't know how it had happened, but somehow Finn was back in his life. And Sydney . . . he didn't know what to think about her anymore. He didn't like her, right?

So why was he so worried about her?

Native Healing

Dakotah sat next to her daughter while she slept. Pancreatitis, the doctor had diagnosed, and they were waiting for some lab work to come back.

There was an IV in Sydney's arm that had just been used to give her medication to take the pain away. Under her hospital gown was her medicine bag. Sydney hadn't let the nurse remove it, and the nurse had backed off her request as soon as Dakotah explained its importance to Sydney and their culture. Everything Sydney held dear to her was in that little bag.

Dakotah glanced over at Sydney and frowned. She couldn't believe this had happened. She had asked the doctor, and he'd told her it could be hereditary, which made sense since Roger had issues with his pancreas.

Speaking of Roger, she should probably call him.

Dakotah got up and walked over to the window to dial his number on her cell phone. He answered on the third ring.

"Hello?"

"It's Dakotah."

"Oh, hi. What's up?"

"Sydney is in the hospital with pancreatitis."

"What? Which hospital? I'll be right there."

"Roger, you can't come. You have supervised visitation and are not allowed to see her outside of that."

"The court will just have to make allowances," he said. "This is an emergency."

"I think she will be fine. She just needs to get her blood count down to normal. It may take a few days."

"I want to see her," said Roger, his voice getting loud now. "I'm on my way."

"They won't let you in," Dakotah pointed out. "She's in the children's unit. They know you aren't allowed to see her."

"Why is that? Did you tell them?"

"Of course. I am required to do so by law."

"You just don't want me to see her. I'm coming anyway."

Dakotah heard a click, and then he was gone. Dakotah sighed and shoved the phone into her back pocket. She left the room and headed down the hall toward the nurse's station.

After Dakotah explained the situation there, the nurse quickly called security, and within minutes, the three of them were making a plan for Roger's arrival. It was decided Roger would be stopped as he got off the elevator by the officer, who would have another officer with him. Roger would be escorted out of the building. If he put up a fuss, Sydney would not hear it, as her room was on the other side of the connecting walkway.

"He will be asked to leave," the officer said. "We'll make sure he drives out of the lot and he doesn't come back."

Dakotah nodded. "Thank you."

"Shut your phone off, ma'am," the officer advised. "If he can't get in, he will be upset and call you. Since I am assuming you will be going back into the room with your daughter, she doesn't need to hear your conversation with him. When you are ready to leave, have the nurse call down to the security desk, and we'll walk you out."

"All right," said Dakotah, relieved now.

She walked back to her daughter's room and shut off her phone before she went inside. Sydney was still asleep.

Her daughter's white flowered hospital gown looked bright next to her dark skin and hair. Dakotah's breath caught in her throat as she took in how delicate her daughter looked just lying there.

She glanced around the stark room and wondered if she should go get some flowers from the gift shop. Other than the necessary medical stuff, the room was empty. Sydney's clothes were put away in the closet, except for her white moccasins, which sat on the floor next to it because Sydney didn't want them out of her sight. Roger had made them for her, and Nokomis had beaded them.

Dakotah reached down and picked up a large tote bag next to the chair she had been sitting in. She opened it and pulled out the four sacred medicines: tobacco, sweetgrass, sage, and cedar.

She knew she couldn't burn anything in the hospital room and felt the spirits knew this too. She placed the tobacco on the table next to Sydney and laid the other plants around it. She knew the tobacco had a special relationship with all plants and would help activate the plant spirits. And a request made with tobacco was special and sacred.

She started to pray, and when she was finished, she quietly sang a beautiful healing song in Ojibwa. Then she bent down and gave Sydney a kiss on the forehead before she sat back down in the chair.

It was going to be a long couple of days, but it looked as though Sydney was going to be all right. Dakotah had already called her boss, who had tried to be understanding about her need to be gone for a few days. She did ask if Dakotah was able to do any remote work, as she really needed her to finish the project they had been working on. Dakotah didn't think the request was appropriate under the circumstances, but she didn't want her boss to assign the project to someone else.

She wondered how she could get her laptop without leaving the hospital. She didn't want to leave Sydney, and she knew once Roger was removed from the hospital, he would be camped out at her house, figuring she would have to come home sometime. She didn't want to see him.

She glanced at her watch to see it was almost three o'clock. School would be out soon. Maybe if she called the office and asked to talk to Finn, she could tell him where the key was, and he could go in and get her laptop. Then maybe his dad would bring it to the hospital . . .

"Mom?"

Dakotah looked over to see her daughter awake now.

"Hi, honey. How are you feeling?" Dakotah reached over to pull the covers up over Sydney's shoulders and gave her a smile.

"Okay, I guess. I still feel icky."

Dakotah smiled. "That's to be expected. Just rest, honey, and you'll be able to go home in a few days."

"The doctor said it could be longer than that," said Sydney. "He said my numbers might take a while to go back down."

"I know, but we'll hope for the best."

Sydney nodded and then turned over to face her. She saw the thoughtful look on her mother's face and asked about it.

"Oh, it's nothing," said her mother.

"Mom . . ."

"Well, my boss was fine with me taking a few days off so I can be with you."

"That's good."

"But she wondered if I could do some remote work to finish a project we've been working on."

"She wants you to work while you're at the hospital with me?" asked Sydney. "How is that getting time off?"

"I would be paid then and not taking time off," replied her mother. "I would just be working from home, basically."

"I see. Well, what do you want to do?"

Dakotah shrugged. "I could work while you sleep," she said. "The problem is, I don't have my laptop." She glanced over at Sydney. "Do you think Finn's dad would be willing to drive him over and get it and then drop it off at the hospital?"

Sydney looked away. "Finn and I aren't talking right now."

"Why?"

"I did something to upset him, and he is angry at me."

"Can I ask what you did?"

Sydney sighed. "I talked to Jeremy about why he wasn't friends with Finn anymore. They used to be best friends, and when Jeremy figured out Finn was gay, he wanted nothing to do with him. It hurt Finn, Mom. I was just trying to see if I could make it better between them."

"Why was Finn mad about that?"

"Because the conversation didn't turn out well. Jeremy went to Finn at school, and they got into an argument. The teachers jumped in, and Jeremy got in trouble again." Sydney looked down at her bed covers. "Finn thinks I betrayed his trust by going to see Jeremy in the first place."

"So, basically, you stuck your nose in someplace it didn't belong?" asked Dakotah. "Now what?"

"I don't know. They're both mad at me, I guess."

"Well, that shoots down the idea of getting the laptop."

Dakotah sat back as the door opened and the nurse stepped in. She gestured for Dakotah to come to the door.

"The dad issue has been taken care of," the nurse whispered in hushed tones.

"Good."

"And there are two boys outside of the unit to see Sydney."

"What? Who?"

The nurse whispered again as Sydney closed her eyes to rest. Her mother glanced at her and then nodded.

"Yes, they have my permission to come in," said Dakotah.

"Usually, we don't let anyone in but family . . ."

"They basically are family," replied Dakotah, hoping she was doing the right thing. "I will meet them outside the door to talk with them before they go inside. They will only be here a few minutes."

The nurse nodded reluctantly and left.

Dakotah stood outside Sydney's room and shook her head. She knew where Sydney got the part of her that always wanted to fix things. Now *she* was sticking her nose in someplace it didn't belong.

A Change Is in the Air

F inn and Jeremy walked silently down the hall toward Sydney's room. As they approached, they saw Dakotah standing outside in the hall. She gestured for them to step away from the door.

"I understand what went down," she said in a quiet voice. "But if you're here to yell at her, you can both go back the way you came."

Pain crossed Finn's face as he dropped his head. "I should have never yelled at her," he whispered. "She was only trying to help me." He lifted his head and added, "Please let me see her. She's my best friend. She's my only friend. If something happens to her . . ." His voice broke as it dropped away.

Finn's words hit Jeremy like a ton of bricks. Sydney was Finn's only friend . . .

Dakotah nodded sympathetically and then glanced over at Jeremy. "What are you doing here?"

He shuffled his feet and looked away. "I don't know," he admitted. "My mom drove us here."

"Why?"

"I asked her to."

"Again, why are you here?"

Jeremy didn't answer, and Finn turned to look at him. He and Dakotah could see the play of emotions running over Jeremy's face. They immediately came to the same conclusion, but by the looks of things, Jeremy hadn't figured it out yet.

Dakotah sighed, then walked over to her daughter's room and pushed the door open. Finn stepped inside, with Jeremy following reluctantly behind.

Finn caught his breath when he saw Sydney. Even Jeremy was taken aback at how sick she looked.

He still couldn't figure out what he was doing there. Earlier, he'd had a hard time explaining to his mother why he was doing anything at all for Sydney and Finn. The whole thing was confusing.

Finn approached the bed and laid a hand on Sydney's cheek. Her eyes fluttered open, and she smiled when she saw him. A moment later, her lips trembled, and her face scrunched up as she started to cry.

"I'm so sorry, Finn," she whispered. "I never meant to hurt you."

Finn carefully dropped down on the bed and put his head down on hers.

"No, it's my fault," he said, tears in his eyes. "I didn't know what I was doing, pushing you away like that."

They reached out to hold each other, and Finn pulled her close, careful of all the tubing in her arm.

Jeremy's eyes filled with guilt, and for the first time, he realized what he had done to these two people. He watched Sydney draw her friend close, and as she closed her eyes, he caught sight of the bruise on her cheek. He dropped his head in shame.

"I love you, Syd," Finn said, and Sydney nodded.

"I love you too," she whispered back, and everyone in the room heard it.

Guilt-ridden, Jeremy stood at the foot of Sydney's bed. He couldn't bear to look at them. He was responsible for their pain.

Jeremy turned to go as Finn pulled back. Sydney's words stopped them both.

"Jeremy?" she asked. "Why are you here?"

He shook his head and started to go, but once again, Sydney's words stopped him.

"Don't leave. I want to talk to you, and I don't want to have to get up and chase you down."

Jeremy sighed. Facing her and Finn now, he struggled to find something to say.

"You look better," he said, and she shook her head.

"No, I don't," she replied. "I look like—"

"Sydney!"

Sydney grinned. "Sorry, Mom." She turned to stare at Jeremy again. "Can I have a moment with Jeremy?"

Dakotah shook her head. "I don't think that's a good idea," she said.

Sydney glanced over at Finn, and he sighed. Standing up, he shoved his hands in his front pockets.

"I would like to buy Sydney something from the gift shop," he said to Dakotah. "Would you go down and help me pick something out?"

"I don't want to leave them alone," replied Dakotah in a hushed tone.

"Mom, really. What do you think is going to happen with me in a hospital bed?" said Sydney. "I mean, look at me," she added, raising the arm with the IV in it. "I just want to talk to Jeremy a moment."

Dakotah didn't like this one bit, but the look in her daughter's eyes said the conversation was going to get heated, and she didn't want to upset her daughter.

She looked over at Jeremy. "I will only be gone a few minutes," she said, and he nodded. Finn sighed, and he and Dakotah left the room.

Alone with Sydney now, Jeremy didn't know what to do. He watched her adjust her gown and then pull her covers up a little farther. Then she gestured to the chair next to her bed.

"Sit."

For a moment, he didn't move. Then, catching the look on her face, he walked over and dropped into the chair.

When she didn't speak right away, he cleared his throat. "Ah . . . you look good, considering," he said, glancing down at his hands. "When are they springing you out of here?"

"In a few days, hopefully."

"Good."

"Jeremy, why are you here?"

"I don't know."

There was silence for a moment, and then he turned to look at her.

"What do you think about me being here?" he asked, and she shrugged.

"I don't know," she responded back, and he smiled.

"I guess we're both in the same boat then," he said.

"Jeremy, I'm sorry about our last conversation . . ."

"I know."

"I never meant to get into your business. But Finn is my friend, and he was hurting."

Jeremy didn't respond for a moment. Then he turned to look at her.

"You go all out for your friends, don't you?" he asked.

She nodded.

"You go all out for everyone," he added. "I mean, you went all out for me, and I'm not even your friend."

"You could be."

Jeremy looked away and shook his head.

"I'm sorry you don't like me," said Sydney, "but I guess I understand why."

Jeremy laughed, and Sydney frowned at the look on his face.

"I don't know why you find that so funny," snapped Sydney, hurt now. "You're a jack—"

"I know," he said, holding up a hand to stop her. "I'm not laughing at you. I'm laughing at myself."

"I don't understand."

"I just realized why I'm here."

"Which is?"

Jeremy sighed. "You drive me nuts. You're a know-it-all, sarcastic, nosy, pushy, hard-headed woman who won't listen to anyone . . ."

"Okay, well, thank you very much," said Sydney stiffly. "You can go now."

"But I like you. I don't know why, but I do."

"You like me?"

"Yup."

"What do you mean you like me?"

He shrugged. "I'm not sure yet."

"Okay, well, this is a stupid conversation," she said, waving her hand toward the door. "You can go now."

Jeremy frowned. "You don't get to tell me what to do all the time," he said firmly. "There have to be some rules here."

"Rules for what?"

"Some kind of relationship," he answered, getting a little loud now.

Sydney frowned. "What are you talking about? You mean a friendship?"

"I don't know yet. But you aren't going to boss me around anymore, do you hear me?"

"The whole hospital can hear you," said Sydney, glancing at the door. "Calm down."

"Well?"

"Well, what?"

He took in a breath to calm himself down and then stared at her. "Do you like me or not?"

"What?"

"Come on, this isn't a math quiz."

"I don't understand," said Sydney, frowning.

"Yes, you do. Don't play stupid."

"Are you calling me stupid?"

"No!" said Jeremy, too loud again. "Just answer the question."

The door opened, and Finn and Dakotah walked back in. They took one look at Sydney and Jeremy and knew they had come back too early.

The silence in the room was deafening and lasted too long. Everyone was staring at Sydney, who was staring at Jeremy.

"We brought you some flowers," said Finn, moving to put them on the table across the room.

"Thanks," Sydney mumbled, still staring at Jeremy.

"Ah, we'd better go," said Finn to Jeremy. "Your mom is in the car waiting, remember?"

Jeremy nodded, and with one last look at Sydney, he turned to go.

"Jeremy?"

He turned to glance back at Sydney.

"Yes," she answered, "I do . . . very much."

"Really?" He gave her a big smile as she nodded. Their eyes held for a moment, and then he turned to Finn.

"Let's go," he said.

With one more glance at Dakotah, Finn reached down to hug Sydney gently.

"I hope you know what you're doing," he whispered to her, and she nodded.

"Me too," she whispered back.

Finn and Jeremy walked to the door and opened it up.

"See you tomorrow?" asked Finn, talking to Dakotah.

"Yes, that's fine," she answered, glancing over at Sydney.

As they walked down the hall toward the elevator, Finn glanced at Jeremy. "If you hurt her, I will kick your—"

Jeremy nodded. "I know. I won't."

They stopped at the elevator, and Finn caught Jeremy's gaze.

"I'm not kidding around," he said.

"Neither am I."

Finn stared at him as the door opened, and then they stepped inside.

An Understanding

A week passed before Sydney was released. She was still weak and tired, so she stayed home from school for a few more days. Finn came over every day after school and brought her homework, and they did it together.

The subject of Jeremy was not discussed. He was no longer coming to the house to work, and he left Finn alone at school. Finn wondered if he had tried to contact Sydney and was waiting for her to bring it up. He wasn't really sure where their relationship was headed. If she befriended Jeremy, it would make things very uncomfortable for Finn.

Dakotah told Sydney about her father trying to see her at the hospital. Roger wouldn't leave on his own and had to be escorted out of the building and out of the lot. The security people had cameras and noticed right away that Roger tried to return twice. Both times he was met in the lot and told to leave. It wasn't until the police were called that Roger finally gave up and left.

Unfortunately, all that was reported to the court. It looked like Roger was going to be denied his appeal on visitation rights. And Dakotah told him he could no longer come to the house to see anyone there. He was very angry and had tried to leave several messages on Dakotah's phone. She ended up blocking his number after he called her eleven times in one day. That was also reported to the courts.

Sydney took all this and tucked it away in her heart, acknowledging that she had been right about him and his apology. It made her sad, but it looked as though he wouldn't be a part of her life right now.

That afternoon, Sydney was feeling well enough to sit outside on the patio. She wrapped herself in a blanket and sat in a lawn chair. The yard looked nice, and some of the fall flowers were still in bloom. The little Three Sisters garden was flourishing, and it was almost ready for harvest.

Sydney loved this time of year, when the air was cool and crisp and the apple trees were full, ready to be picked. Hopefully they would be able to get to the orchard soon for Honey Crisp apples and apple slushies.

Sighing, she closed her eyes as a cloud blew by quickly to allow some sun to shine through.

She had lost some weight, and she knew she didn't look her best at the moment. She still felt tired out and weak and was glad her mother had let her have a few more days off before going back to school. She didn't really feel like facing Jeremy looking and feeling like this.

"So, this is what you're skipping school for?"

Sydney opened her eyes to see Jeremy drop down in a chair beside her. She groaned inwardly and closed her eyes, trying to wish him away.

She hadn't seen or spoken to him since that day in the hospital when he said he liked her. Many times she'd wondered why he hadn't come over to see her after she had been released. She'd started to wonder if she had imagined the conversation with him. After all, she had been on pain medication.

But now he was here, sitting next to her. She opened her eyes and sighed. Stretching, she pulled the blanket around her again.

He reached out and tucked it in under her chin, and their eyes met. Slowly he pulled his hand away and sat back.

"Where have you been?" asked Sydney.

"Around," answered Jeremy with a shrug. "Why? Did you miss me?"

Sydney snorted and turned away, studying the big tree at the back of the yard.

When she didn't answer, he shook his head. "My mother would call you persnickety," he commented, leaning back and crossing one leg over the other.

Sydney rolled her eyes. "My mother would call you bagwanawizi."

"Which means?"

Sydney smiled. "Do you really want to know?"

Jeremy leaned forward and looked at the ground. "I don't know. Do I?" he asked.

When he looked up, his green eyes caught hers, and for a moment, neither looked away.

"What are you doing here?" she asked.

"I wanted to be sure you were all right."

"Why?"

"Because I like you, remember?"

"Yeah, about that. I—"

"Nope."

"What?" asked Sydney.

He sat back in the chair. "I'm not going to let you pick that apart."

"Pick what apart?"

Jeremy sighed. "How much I like you, how much you like me, why I like you, why you like me, does it mean anything, where are we going with this . . ."

"Okay, I get it," replied Sydney. "Who said I was going to do that?"

"Weren't you?"

Sydney snorted again and looked away. Jeremy smiled.

"Have you talked to Finn?" asked Sydney, changing the subject.

Jeremy shook his head.

"Why?"

Jeremy shrugged. "Don't want to."

"Are you gay?"

"What? No," said Jeremy. "Why would you think that?"

"I don't."

"Then why ask me that?"

"You talked to Finn a week ago. Maybe his 'gayness' rubbed off on you."

"Yeah, right," said Jeremy. "That's not going to happen."

"No, it's not," agreed Sydney. "So there was no reason not to talk to him."

Jeremy was silent for a moment. He looked away, seeing the lawn and the bushes he had worked so hard on over the past several weeks.

"Your yard looks good," he said, glancing at her. "But I bet this is not what you're used to. It probably looks nothing like the reservation."

"You're very good at that," said Sydney.

"What?"

"Moving the conversation away from things you don't want to talk about."

"I get lots of practice at home."

Sydney nodded. "I understand. I'm sorry you have to do that."

Jeremy smiled. "Thanks. But it's mostly my fault. My parents are not thrilled with my behavior at school."

"Why don't you change it?"

"I don't know who I am without it."

Sydney stared at him. "That's very profound."

He smiled. "Yeah, I hit the mark once in a while." He looked away. "But my counselor told me that a couple of weeks ago."

"You see a counselor?"

He nodded.

"No one knows that, do they?" asked Sydney.

He shook his head.

Sydney sat up, swinging her legs around and throwing off the blanket. She pushed her hair back behind her ears and sighed. "Look, I get what you're saying. But you're mean to people. You bully them. I know you have your reasons, but you have to stop before it takes over your life and you end up losing everything."

Jeremy turned to face her. "What are you talking about? You don't know anything about where I'm at, and—"

"Yes, I do."

"What?"

Sydney sighed. "I was a bully when I lived on the reservation." She looked away. "That's still a part of me."

"What do you mean?"

"I was mean to people," she replied. "Well, one person in particular. Pushing people around made me feel better."

"You pushed her?"

"I bullied with words, bagwanawizi."

He sat back. "Stop calling me that," he said. "I don't know what it means, and I don't like it."

Sydney stared at him for a moment and then sighed. "I'm sorry. It means you're stupid, and you're not."

Sydney leaned back against the lawn chair and pulled the blanket over her again.

"You were a bully?" asked Jeremy. "I can't picture it. You're so sweet and kind to people."

Sydney gave him a smile, and Jeremy realized how pretty she really was. He cleared his throat and looked away.

"I mean, it's hard to picture you as a bully," he said.

"Thanks. I see those things in you as well."

"What? How?" he asked, frowning. "I have been nothing but awful to you and Finn. I even punched you in the face."

"Yeah, that wasn't so great, but I always knew there was more to you than what you put out there."

Jeremy didn't speak for a moment. No one had ever bothered to look that deep before. Only he knew "The Bully" was just a protective shield for the pain he carried around inside him. *Get people before they get you,* he thought. *It keeps you safe and always in control.*

He glanced over at Sydney. She seemed to know somehow. She had seen beyond his behavior when no one else had ever bothered to give him a second look.

Sydney gazed back at him, seeing conflicting thoughts in his eyes. She took his hand and smiled.

"We're the same, you and me," she said quietly. "Ninjichaag and gijichaag."

"What does that mean?" he whispered, gazing back at her.

"My soul and your soul. They know each other."

He nodded, spellbound by her eyes and her words.

Sydney smiled. "I could use some help working on myself," she said. "Maybe we could help each other be kinder to ourselves and others."

He gave her a skeptical look. "Maybe. I'm willing to give it a go."

Tears filled her eyes as she pulled her hand out of his. "And then maybe I can forgive myself for the way I treated someone who didn't deserve all the crap I gave her."

Jeremy caught his breath, not knowing what to do.

"Hey, stop . . . don't cry," he pleaded. "I don't know how to fix that. It's going to be okay." He took her hand again and gave it a squeeze.

She looked over at him with shimmery eyes, and he couldn't help himself. He leaned over and kissed her softly on the cheek and then pulled away. When he saw the look she was giving him, he threw caution to the wind and reached out again, cupping her face this time.

His kiss was gentle, and she closed her eyes when she saw that he had. A moment later, Jeremy pulled back and slowly dropped his hands.

"Was that okay?" he asked, not looking at her.

She smiled and nodded. "I thought it was better than okay."

He smiled. "I need to go now," he said. "My mom has some work for me to do at home."

"Okay," replied Sydney, disappointment in her eyes.

He laughed. "I'll call you later if you give me your number."

He held out his phone, and she entered her number into it. He took it back and shoved it into his back pocket.

"See you tomorrow," he said.

"Really?" she asked hopefully, and he laughed.

"Of course," he replied.

He got up, and she watched him walk away. After he had gotten a few feet away, he paused and turned around.

"Sydney?"

"Yes."

"I think the trick to all this is trying to see ourselves the way we see each other," he said.

"That's easier said than done."

"Isn't it though."

With a nod, he left.

Sydney smiled and sat back in the chair and closed her eyes. Ten minutes later, she was asleep.

Dakotah was doing the dishes and had seen and heard everything through the window in front of her. When Jeremy reached out to kiss her daughter, she had grabbed a towel to go out there, but stopped herself. If she wanted her daughter to be able to handle the grown-up stuff, she had to let her be.

She didn't know what to think. Both Sydney and Jeremy had control issues, and this could end very badly for everyone involved. Or they could end up helping each other.

She sighed, setting down the dish scrubber. She glanced up at the sky through the window.

Gitchie Manitou would be getting some very specific prayers tonight.

An Air of Peace

Sydney smudged her bedroom by lighting sage and letting it burn for a moment before blowing it out. She smiled as she picked up the herb's earthy fragrance as she moved it around the room. She was starting to feel better already and looked forward to moving forward in her life. Grandmother always said smudging was the best way to clear out old energy and invite new energy in.

A few months had gone by since she had gotten sick, and now she felt like her old self again. A lot of not-so-great stuff had happened within her personal life, and she felt the need to put it all behind her and move on.

Her father had dropped his request to see her unsupervised. As a matter of fact, he made the decision to stop seeing her period. When Sydney was told about it, she cried. She loved her father and missed him very much. But she understood his need for time to get his life back on track and to focus on himself. She just hoped that he hadn't written her out of his life forever.

Trying to make Sydney feel better about things, her mother had rented a house in St. Petersburg, Florida, for their vacation. After the year they'd had, they decided to plan absolutely nothing for the four days they were there. Sydney already had books she was bringing to read and a brand-new pair of sandals her mother had bought her.

Thinking about them now, she picked up her pair of white moccasins, smudged them, and put them in the closet. They were getting too small for her, and she felt if she put them away, it would help her begin to let go of the father who made them. She had thought if she wore them every day, he would see how much she really loved him, but it hadn't made a difference. He had still criticized her and made her feel small. Maybe he would change, maybe she would forgive him, and maybe things would get better between them. But maybe not. Either way, she had to figure out a way to let go of "yesterday's rain," as her grandmother called it, and look toward the future.

"Stop looking behind you," her grandmother would say. "You're not going that way."

Nokomis was the wisest person Sydney knew. Her kitchen always smelled like herbs and spices, as well as berries and wild rice. She loved to cook and had taught Sydney several wild rice dishes and how to cook the traditional way.

Sydney wished for the hundredth time that they hadn't moved so far away from the reservation and Nokomis. Her mom had tried to get Nokomis to move with them, but she was set in her traditional ways and refused to leave her home. Both Sydney and her mother understood that and didn't push her any further, but they both missed her very much.

Nokomis would have liked Finn and Jeremy, mused Sydney, setting the sage bundle down on the abalone shell and sitting cross-legged on the bed.

Finn had started looking at colleges. He thought maybe a community college would be a good way to start, as he couldn't decide on a major. Sydney had no idea what she was going to do, and for a while, that had bothered her. But her mother told her she had plenty of time to decide, and that made her feel better.

Jeremy was such a good football player; he was on the high school football team. He had colleges scouting him, and for him it would just be a question of where he wanted to go.

His grades were crap, though, as he told Sydney many times. He had to get them up or he wouldn't even be accepted into a college. She had started helping him, but he hated schoolwork, and it had been a rough road. There had been many times Sydney had thrown her hands up in defeat as he once again raged on and on about how stupid he was. He challenged Sydney to think of different ways to help him, and she had been creative in doing so. Even Jeremy begrudgingly acknowledged her hard work.

"Thanks," he said, getting another math problem done. "I don't know why you put up with me."

"Me either," she said, smiling.

Their relationship was a rocky one. They were both headstrong and always thought they were right. It was a contest to see who could yell the loudest, and some days Dakotah had to step in to calm things down. But it was clear to see Jeremy needed her daughter, and her daughter had feelings for him. The way Sydney looked at him was enough to make Dakotah back off from stopping the relationship.

Jeremy had never touched her roughly again. Unbeknownst to Dakotah, he had cried once when talking to Sydney about having hurt her. Sydney knew then he was truly sorry, and had hugged him to calm him down. She felt he would never again hurt her.

Her life was going pretty well at the moment, except for her issues with Amelia and her friends. Although they had never again confronted her, they had been spreading rumors about the nature of her and Finn's relationship. Amelia was livid when she found out Jeremy and Sydney were dating. Turns out, Amelia had a little crush on Jeremy.

Sydney got up and looked out her bedroom window, which faced the backyard. She smiled when she saw her mother with her light brown straw hat on, leaning against the fence around the little garden.

Knowing her mother was waiting for her, Sydney left her room and padded barefoot down the hall. She walked out the back door, grabbing some gardening gloves and putting them on. Then she headed to the other side of the yard, where the garden was.

"Come on over," said her mother. "I'm ready to get started."

As Sydney walked toward her mother, her eyes grew big as Finn and Jeremy stepped over to stand beside her mother. Jeremy had on a hat that made him look like a farmer, while Finn had a backward baseball hat on his head.

"We thought we'd help out," said Jeremy with a grin. "How do I look?" He was wearing a pair of brown overalls and gardening gloves that were a little too small.

She shook her head and glanced at Finn. He had found some old black rain boots and wore those with a pair of ripped-up jeans and a T-shirt. He had on no gloves.

"I wanted to feel the dirt under my nails," he declared, holding out his hands in front of him.

Dakotah shook her head. "He wants to feel the cuts on his hands from the corn leaves," she added, glancing down at the Three Sisters planting of beans, corn, and squash.

Suddenly, a cloud burst open, and they were getting drenched from a sun shower. They all ran for the tree near the garden to wait it out.

Jeremy reached down to take Sydney's hand. Finn, unaware of this and on the other side of her, grabbed the other one. Sydney gave them both a squeeze and silently thanked Gitchie Manitou for all the blessings in her life.

As she stood there, she remembered an old Ojibwa prayer her grandmother had taught her.

May you be strengthened by yesterday's rain, walk straight in tomorrow's wind, and cherish each moment of the sun today.

Sydney smiled as she glanced at Jeremy and Finn. She felt her life was finally about to turn a corner, and she was ready.

RESOURCES

PACER'S NATIONAL BULLYING PREVENTION CENTER

pacer.org/bullying

PACER's National Bullying Prevention Center actively leads social change to prevent childhood bullying so that all youth are safe and supported in their schools, communities, and online. PACER provides innovative resources for students, parents, educators, and others, and recognizes bullying as a serious community issue that negatively affects education, physical and emotional health, and the safety and well-being of students.

COMMITTEE FOR CHILDREN

cfchildren.org/programs/bullying-prevention

Committee for Children helps empower kids and the adults around them by supplying information and resources to understand what bullying is, who is affected by it, and what the community can do to prevent it.

NATIONAL ASSOCIATION OF ELEMENTARY SCHOOL PRINCIPALS

naesp.org/bullying-prevention-resources

Maintaining a safe, nurturing school environment for students is any school leader's top priority. The resources provided by NAESP can help principals and teachers combat bullying in their schools.

StopBullying.gov

StopBulling.gov provides information from various government agencies on what bullying is, what cyberbullying is, who is at risk, and the best ways to prevent and respond to bullying.

AMERICAN ACADEMY OF CHILD & ADOLESCENT PSYCHIATRY
Bullying Resource Center

aacap.org/AACAP/Families_and_Youth/Resource_Centers/Bullying_Resource_Center/Home.aspx

Child and adolescent psychiatrists are trained to look out for signs that a child is the victim of bullying. They can help concerned parents take the proper plan of action to make sure their children get all the support they need to stay resilient and confident.

THE LGBT NATIONAL HOTLINE

glbthotline.org/hotline.html

The LGBT hotline provides a safe, anonymous, and confidential space where callers can speak on many different issues and concerns, including coming out, gender and/or sexuality identity, bullying, and much more.

STOMP OUT BULLYING

stompoutbullying.org/helpchat

The goal of the STOMP Out Bullying live HelpChat Line is to help reduce the stress, depression, and fear that can result from being bullied and to empower those who have been bullied to make healthy decisions.

ABOUT THE AUTHOR

KIM SIGAFUS is an award-winning Ojibwa writer and Illinois Humanities Road Scholar speaker. She has coauthored two 7th Generation books in the Native Trailblazers series of biographies, including *Native Elders: Sharing Their Wisdom* and the award-winning *Native Writers: Voices of Power*. Her fiction work includes the PathFinders novels *Nowhere to Hide*, *Autumn's Dawn*, and *Finding Grace*, which are the first three books in the Autumn Dawn series, and The Mida, an eight-volume series about a mystically powerful time-traveling carnival owned by an Ojibwa woman. Kim's family is from the White Earth Indian Reservation in northern Minnesota. She resides with her husband in Freeport, Illinois. For more information, visit kimberlysigafus.com.

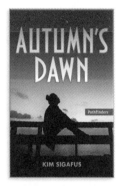